Metis
Spirits

Metis Spirits

Deborah L. Delaronde

PEMMICAN
PUBLICATIONS
INC.

Pemmican Publications gratefully acknowledges the assistance accorded to its publishing program by the Manitoba Arts Council, the Province of Manitoba - Department of Culture, Heritage and Tourism, Canada Council for the Arts and Canadian Heritage - Book Publishing Industry Development Program.

Printed and Bound in Canada
First Printing: 2006

Library and Archives Canada Cataloguing in Publication

Delaronde, Deborah L., 1958-
        Metis spirits / written by Deborah L. Delaronde.

ISBN 1-894717-36-8

        1. Métis--Juvenile fiction. I. Title.

PS8557.E4254M48 2006   jC813'.54   C2006-906336-2

PEMMICAN
PUBLICATIONS
INC.

Pemmican Publications Inc.
Committed to the promotion of Metis culture and heritage

150 Henry Ave., Winnipeg, Manitoba, R3B 0J7, Canada
www.pemmican.mb.ca

Dedicated to Future Metis Spirit Fiddlers

This story is commemorative to Metis fiddlers both past and present. With the passing of time, the spirit of the Metis Fiddlers was almost lost. Thanks to Frontier School Division and all fiddling instructors for providing the opportunity of learning to play the fiddle to thousands of young Metis who now preserve this.

The spirit lives on.

CONTENTS

METIS SPIRITS

THE EERIE AND HAUNTING MELODY FILTERED
by the breeze flowed faintly through the air.
It touched softly upon the ears and the hearts
of the two weary travelers.

Joey frowned, turning his ear to the sound,
seeking its location.

"I thought you said nobody has lived in
this area for years?" Joey asked, turning to
his companion.

"You can hear that music?" Angus
asked, amazed.

Joey said hopefully, "Maybe campers
or hunters!

"Quick, let's find it before it stops!" he
said as they scrambled through thick grass
and underbrush.

They stopped for a brief moment to listen to the music, until they came upon a clearing.

Shocked yet relieved, the boys stopped and stood staring at a young man playing a fiddle and stepping in time to his fiddle tune.

As they walked slowly toward the fiddler, they cautiously looked around for the young man's traveling companions.

Joey cleared his throat.

It was as though an electric shock had gone through the fiddle player. The silence was deafening until the young man blinked his eyes in disbelief and said, "Are you real? You're not spirits, are you?"

Joey and Angus sighed, and shrugged their shoulders with relief.

"We were thinking the same thing about you," Angus said.

"Strange things have been seen in this forest," the fiddler explained.

"Are you alone or are you traveling with anyone?" Joey asked.

"My village is not far from here," the fiddler replied, pointing north.

"My name is Patrick," he said, smiling and holding his hand out in greeting.

"What would two fine fellows such as yourselves be doing in this area of the woods?" he asked, shaking hands with the boys.

"I'm Joey, and this is my friend, Angus," Joey replied. "We were traveling with a group of friends following a bush trail when we got separated. We've been wandering for a few days, feeding on wild berries when we can find them.

"Would your family mind terribly if we mooched a meal and phoned to let our families know we're okay?" Joey asked.

"Not at all," Patrick said. "We don't get visitors very often."

As they walked to the village, Joey asked, "I hope you don't mind my asking, but why were you playing your fiddle in the field?"

"Oh, haaahh!" Patrick laughed. "We are a village of fiddle makers. Every time a fiddle is made, we go to the clearing to tune and test it.

"There's something about the forest that brings out the purest sounds of a freshly crafted fiddle," he explained seriously.

Joey and Angus had been so intent on listening to Patrick's explanation that they hadn't realized that they had already passed several houses.

"Here's my home," Patrick said.

"It's not the best cabin in town, but good enough when you're roughing it in the bush," he said as they stepped inside.

Only then did Joey and Angus stop to look around and see that all the houses were log cabins.

"This is either a historic site or a cult of some kind," Joey whispered as they followed Patrick into the cabin. "Act normal. Pretend you don't notice."

The smell of freshly cut wood mixed with the aroma of a stew and baked bannock stirred their temporarily forgotten hunger. Soon Joey and Angus were wolfing down mouthfuls of sopping bannock dunked in moose stew.

Patrick watched with an amused expression as the two ate.

"Are you sure you were lost in the bush for only two days?" he asked.

"Seems that you're in any condition to walk any further."

The rest of the meal was spent in silence as Patrick began working on his next fiddle project. Joey and Angus watched as he cut the back part of the fiddle following a pattern marked on the wood.

"This is a beautiful fiddle," Joey said as he picked up the fiddle Patrick had been testing.

"Would you like to learn how to make your own fiddle?" Patrick asked.

"Why not?" Joey shrugged. "It looks like we're going to have a bit of time while we wait."

"A maple log was brought to us by a voyageur friend," Patrick explained.

"The pattern pieces are already cut," Patrick continued. "I've never tried to make a fiddle from waterlogged maple before. Maple trees don't grow very well this far north. For this particular fiddle, the back and rib pieces as well as the scroll and neck were made using a maple log. The top plate, however, is made of spruce.

"I'm sure that when you're done, this will be a fiddle worth taking home. All you have to do now is glue it together and apply your varnish."

Time seemed to stand still for Joey and Angus as they worked on the maple wood fiddle together. They learned about fiddle making during the day and practiced learning how to play the fiddle by night.

The days passed by swiftly since the messenger had been sent to town, but neither Joey nor Angus seemed concerned.

Finally, with the last string threaded, the boys spent the day in the field tuning, testing and jigging to Joey's maple fiddle. There couldn't have been a more excellent moment in time as the three celebrated a job well done.

· · · ·

The next day, there was a knock on the door signaling the messenger's return home.

After much whispering, Patrick turned to the boys and said, "We value our way of life and don't want it spoiled by people who wouldn't understand.

"I'll walk you to the clearing where you first saw me. It's been arranged that someone will pick you up there."

At the clearing, as Patrick shook Joey's hand, he presented the fiddle to Joey as a gift.

"It's a fine fiddle," Patrick said proudly. "I'll tune it one more time so you'll never have a problem with it losing its tone.

"In return, I need you to do me just one favour," Patrick said, gazing at Joey with a serious and intent look.

"If I can," Joey replied.

"Please take this fiddle and play it for an audience," Patrick said.

"If you can do that, we will be honoured knowing that you've shared a lifetime's work from the people of my village," he said mysteriously.

Patrick then turned and walked back to the village.

"Today seems to be a day of parting because this is where I leave you as well," Angus said, smiling sadly.

Shocked that Angus would consider such a thing, Joey asked, "What about your family, Angus? They'll be waiting for you."

Ignoring him, Angus continued, "Before you go, Joey, there is something that you should know. Without realizing it, you helped those people back there in the village."

"How?" Joey asked. "It seems more like they helped us."

"We helped you," Angus said. "I was merely a spiritual guide to take you there and then ensure your safe return home. By now you must realize that something strange has happened to you."

Joey shook his head, confused.

· · · ·

"For an instant in time, I took you back to a village that existed over 100 years ago," Angus continued. "It was a fine village of Scottish Metis.

They were excellent craftspeople who were striving to create the purest-sounding fiddles. It was their intention to market their fiddles and make their village respected and noted for its craftsmanship.

"Unfortunately, the voyageur that brought the maple log that was used to cut the pieces for your fiddle also brought smallpox to the Metis. The people never had a chance and perished. They were so far from the nearest settlement that you're the only one who knows that they ever existed.

"My purpose was to recreate the Metis village and people so that you would appreciate their lifestyle and confirm their existence.

"When you wake, this will all seem like a dream. Just remember what Patrick asked of you. He was the real ghost," Angus said as he, too, turned and slowly walked back towards the village.

· · · ·

A loud whirring sound cut through Joey's senses as he woke to a strong wind swirling around his head.

Looking up, he saw a helicopter preparing to land nearby. Joey sat up and waved excitedly.

He turned to the spruce trees to wave and let Angus know that he would be all right. Where the village had been were piles of logs.

"Could these have been the log cabins in the village?"

A shiver ran through his entire body. Joey groaned and lifted his hand to feel for a lump he felt painfully sure was on the back of his head. He then remembered hiking with his friends and following an old bush trail. He had gotten lost, fell and hit his head on something.

"Had it all been a dream caused by the fall?" he wondered.

"It all seemed so real," he whispered in disbelief as he turned to get up from the ground. His hand touched something lying beside him in the grass.

It was the fiddle!

Joey then remembered what Patrick had asked of him. He picked up the fiddle and decided that he would find the right time and the right place to fulfill his promise.

. . . .

Weeks later, Joey stood in front of an audience of Metis people during their annual cultural celebrations.

The eerie and haunting melody flowed through the crowd as Joey began to play his fiddle. The men, women and even the children stopped talking and fidgeting to listen to his fiddle tune. Their smiles of acceptance and pride were all that Joey needed in order to close his eyes and put his heart into his fiddle. As Joey continued to play, he realized that it wasn't the wood that made the fiddle . . . it was the spirit of the Metis!

METIS VIRTUAL MUSEUM

"BEFORE WE GO ANY FURTHER, I NEED TO remind you that there are 'DO NOT TOUCH' signs posted throughout the museum. There are very good reasons for this, so pullleeasse keep your hands to yourselves," Mrs. Granger told the class.

"Museums are sooo boring," Brian said in disgust to his best friend Dave as they straggled behind, trying very hard not to listen.

"What's the sense of seeing if you can't touch?" he whispered.

Dave snickered quietly. "In your case, that could be a problem. From the museum's point of view, if seeing is believing then it's worth preserving.

As they reluctantly joined the rest of the class, Dave's voice lowered to a whisper, "So do me a favour, try to restrain yourself from touching anything."

"We're coming to the Metis exhibit," the museum guide stated when the lights flashed briefly.

"A minor power problem." She paused, looking up at the ceiling nervously. "It happens on occasion."

. . . .

"The origins of the Metis people, or Bois-Brûlés as they were sometimes called began with the arrival of the explorers and the early settlers," she began. "The Metis, as they identified themselves, were a product of their native and European parents. The arrival of the first settlers created a demand for the fur from animals such as the beaver, mink, fox and others in order to survive Canada's winter climate. This created and extended a market for export use in England, France and other countries that found the furs both warm and fashionable.

"As the early settlers arrived, they were often unprepared to survive the long, cold winter months. They learned how to survive in this country from both the native and Metis people. During the 1800s, there was a time when the Metis outnumbered the rest of Canada by as much as 70 per cent," she said.

"It was during these years that the Metis were employed in a number of ways, having acquired the skills from both their native and European parents. The Metis were skilled guides, hunters, trappers and fishermen. They also harvested wild plants and berries according to their seasons, and planted gardens and farmed small acreages. The seasons dictated when it was time to begin and end a particular activity," she said, and paused briefly to clear her throat before beginning again.

"During the early fall, the Metis would gather in large numbers for an annual buffalo hunt. This was a time to work together in order to hunt and process meat to make pemmican. Five pounds of meat would make one pound of pemmican. This food source was light to carry and would keep through the winter months.

"However, there were no roads, but only bush trails all across Canada, so the Metis created a vehicle in which to carry their possessions over rough terrain.

"Pemmican was an important trade item for the Metis. They could use it to trade for food, tools, clothing and other items they considered necessary for their needs and survival," she said as she walked back toward to a wooden structure with floodlights focused on it.

"Please crowd around this special exhibit," the museum guide said.

"The Red River Cart was made entirely of wood," she began again. "There was no mistaking the sound it made as it traveled across the prairies by the high-pitched squealing of wood rubbing against wood. Imagine hundreds of these carts traveling as the Metis went on their annual buffalo hunts."

"I read somewhere that chewing birch bark cured headaches. Imagine everyone chewing on big sticks instead of toothpicks," Dave whispered with a smirk while elbowing Brian in the ribs.

"Maybe that's when toothpicks got invented," Brian whispered back seriously while moving closer towards the cart. "They realized how ridiculous they looked!"

"Look at this!" Brian said, impressed as he reached out his hand to touch the wooden wheel. "This looks like the real thing!"

"DON'T TOUCH!" Dave shouted as he grabbed Brian's jacket to pull him away.

"Don't just touch the wheel boy, LIFT IT!" the woman shouted.

Brian and Dave stood staring at the woman, their mouths opening in shock as their arms fell to their sides!

"One more time," she said in desperation. "We need to get this wheel attached or we'll have to leave everything behind and start walking."

"Oh, I know what this is . . . ," Brian said as he turned and whispered to Dave, who was standing behind him.

"The museum has gone virtual," he smiled and winked. "Just play along."

"What do we do, ma'am?" he asked, emphasizing the last word.

"Just fit the wheel onto the axle," she said.

"And you boy, come here and help us lift the cart," she said to Dave.

With the wheel in place, the woman began pounding a pin in the axle.

"Thank goodness you came along when you did," she said gratefully. "Sorry for yelling at you, but we were getting desperate."

"No problem," Brian said with a smile.

"So, what do we do now?" Brian asked, willing to play along.

"You can travel with us if you'd like. We need extra hands now that my husband has taken sick," she said.

"First, we need to get him back up on the wagon and made comfortable," she said with authority.

"What's wrong with him?" Dave asked, faking concern.

"Nothing that Seneca root or wild ginger won't cure," she replied. "I just need to find more before my supply is used up."

Brian and Dave looked around at their surroundings in the wilderness and then at the family of four: a young girl, a little boy and a mother and father, all out in the middle of nowhere.

"What are you doing here?" Dave asked curiously.

Surprised, the woman turned to the boys.

"The same thing you're doing, I imagine. We're going to the spring buffalo hunt," she said.

"John wasn't feeling well when we left home, with a fever and coughing, so we ended up straggling behind.

"We needed to stop every three hours so I could boil a medicine tea, when the cart hit a rock coming down that hill," she said, pointing in the direction behind them.

"If you'll join up with us, we'll share the pemmican with you," she offered. "This is such an important time of year, as you can imagine. With my husband sick, we are desperate for any help until he gets better and we find our hunting group."

"Sure," Brian said as he turned to face Dave with a knowing smirk. "We're looking for the people we were with, too."

. . . .

They had traveled as long as the sun would allow when the woman, whose name they learned was Mary, called out that it was time to make camp. Who knew that traveling to these people meant taking turns walking and then riding on the cart only when you grew too tired to walk any farther.

Exhausted, the boys helped unload the tent and supplies from the cart, following the children's instructions.

"You're not from around here, are you?" Mary asked.

"We're new to the area," Dave replied. "Actually, we're not sure what we're doing here."

"Maybe you were an answer to our prayers," she said.

"Josh, if you can make a fire, and one of you boys can go get water from the creek, Eleanor will put the kettle to boil. I'll make a stew for supper when I return," she said as she looked around, searching the area.

"Right now, I need to see if I can find a few medicine plants before the sun goes down tonight. I'll see you in a bit," she said as she walked towards the bush.

With the tent set up, thanks largely to Josh and Eleanor, Brian grabbed a wooden pail to get water. Dave and the children then proceeded to gather dry wood to make a fire. Brian struggled back with the pail of water, having slopped it mostly over himself with very little remaining in the pail.

"You might have to make a second trip," Dave laughed. "I don't think there's enough left for a drink of water."

"Well, I guess I'm not used to walking 10 kilometres a day, setting up hide tents and carrying heavy wooden pails of water," Brian said, breathless and with a hint of sarcasm.

"Well . . . what do you think of the tour so far?" Brian asked as he set the pail down.

"Where are the others?" Dave asked, emphasizing the word 'others' while pouring the water into a pot.

"I think I have that figured out," Brian said thoughtfully. "They're all in different virtual realities, either in this same exhibit or in different ones. Who knows, we may come across them yet."

"Hmmm . . . ," Dave said, a bit worried. "I guess we have no choice but to go along and see how this all plays out."

"In virtual-reality games, you usually have to play the game until the end or you win," Brian said. "Admit it, this is sort of fun and exciting."

"I guess," Dave admitted grudgingly.

"If your idea of fun has to do with walking all day 'til your feet are blistered and getting bitten by 10,000 mosquitoes, then yeah!" he added sarcastically.

Just then, Mary returned with plants that she set out to dry near the fire. She then boiled some of the water that Brian had brought, and made a tea, mixing in other ingredients that she extracted from a beaded bag.

When the ingredients were boiled, she carefully poured this mixture into a cup and then went to give it to her husband, John. When he was settled and resting, she returned and with equal care poured the remainder of the fluid into a bag that looked awfully and disgustingly like real skin.

She then poured more water into the pot to boil, cut off a chunk of what looked like brown shoe leather, along with a few misshapen vegetables that she had picked and a sprinkle of some herbs that she carefully unwrapped from another beaded bag.

The aroma of the stew was soon drawing hunger pangs that everyone found entertaining while they sat waiting patiently for the stew to cook.

The only smells that Brian could identify that were familiar to him were the onions and sage.

With the stew cooking at a steady boil, Mary poured some flour into a bowl, and then added a chunk of lard, salt and a few other ingredients. She added some water and mixed this with her hands to form six balls. She set those aside on a flat stone while she cleaned up. With a silent nod to Josh and Eleanor, the children left. They returned shortly with green willow sticks.

She then kneaded each ball into a long strip, wrapped them around each stick and placed them over the fire to bake.

"Better gather enough firewood to last through the night," she said to everyone. "I'll call you when the stew and bannock are done."

While the boys gathered wood, Josh and Eleanor instead collected buffalo dung.

"Burns longer," Josh said, seeing their shocked expressions.

Finally, Mary called them back to camp. "You boys must be hungry," she said. "Care for a plate of Rubaboo?"

"Rub a who?" Brian asked, tasting a spoonful with the tip of his tongue.

"Mmmmm . . . I've never tasted stew this good," he said, and began eating like he hadn't eaten in a week. Following everyone's example, he used his bannock to scrape the plate clean of any remaining gravy.

Mary prepared a plate of stew and bannock and poured another cup of medicine tea for John while everyone else helped clean and pack everything away before climbing into their tent to sleep.

· · · ·

The next morning brought morning dew and a chill so deep that the boys didn't feel like getting up.

Mary and the children were already preparing breakfast. Once again, she boiled first the medicine tea for her husband.

The boys went to the creek to wash and when they returned, plates were set out with the Rubaboo left over from the previous night.

"Waste not, want not," Brian whispered lightheartedly to Dave as they ate what these people apparently called breakfast, dinner and supper.

Just then a roaring sound like thunder could be heard in the distance. Brian and Dave searched the sky for signs of rain clouds, but the sky remained clear. Mary ran quickly to the cart, drew a rifle and handed it to John.

John raised himself on one elbow, squinting his eyes at the sound. Seeing dust, he sat up, loaded the rifle and motioned for Brian to come closer.

"Look for stragglers," he said. "If one should turn away from the herd towards us or if the herd begins to turn our way, shoot," he said breathlessly, with a fit of coughing, and then lay back down weakly on the cart.

The children joined their father.

"Herd of what?" Brian turned and asked Dave.

Grabbing Brian by the arm, Mary guided him to a spot ahead of the cart.

"Get down on one knee, raise the rifle to your shoulder. If one of the buffalo should leave the main herd, use the beaded front sight of the rifle, aim for his shoulder and shoot," she shouted.

Mary instructed Dave to hold the oxen on one side while she positioned herself on the other.

The ground shook as the herd thundered towards them.

Brian saw a rider on horseback in the distance, shooting into the herd. Brian watched, fascinated, as the rider guided his horse with his knees while using both hands to shoot and reload. The rider seemed unaware of their presence as he held his position, running alongside the herd.

Brian desperately tried to remember if anyone ever got hurt or killed while in a virtual game. He made a quick mental note to find out where the museum placed their stop buttons.

He then forced himself to focus on the scene developing in front of him as the ground he was kneeling on shook and trembled. Brian started to shake nervously, but didn't dare turn to get encouragement from Dave.

The herd moved fast. Soon the buffalo were moving along past the small cart group when a rogue bull turned towards them.

"Steady," Mary shouted above the noise. "Don't shoot until he's at least 100 yards."

"Right," Brian thought. *"Now, I have to think metric conversion at a time like this!"*

Mentally, he judged 100 to be equal to roughly 110 metres.

The rogue wasted no time and pounded the ground at a full run towards them.

Time stood still as Brian raised the rifle, braced himself, used the rifle's barrel and lined up the sight to locate the buffalo's shoulder.

As the animal thundered towards him with deadly purpose, Brian thought, *"If I didn't know this was virtual, I'd probably panic and run."*

With the dust and the ground shaking and affecting Brian's aim, he waited until the last possible moment.

The animal was no more than 50 metres away. He heard Mary shouting vaguely when he fired. The force of the rifle firing threw Brian back a few metres.

The animal fell, but continued to move forward with the momentum of its own speed. It rested not 40 metres away from Brian in a cloud of dust. With the shot, the herd veered away from them.

The rider shot at another animal nearby as he thundered past, shouting something and waving his gun at the downed animal and then toward them in a salute.

"That didn't seem virtual," Dave said in disbelief as he joined Brian to look at the fallen buffalo.

"One to eat and one to trade," Brian said as he reached down to touch the buffalo's cape.

"That's probably how it was done," he said as he felt the coarseness of the hair. "A guy could really get into the spirit of this game."

"Brian, Dave . . . there are 'Do Not Touch' signs posted everywhere," Mrs. Granger said sternly as she looked at Brian's hand on the cart.

Brian and Dave blinked and stared at the Mrs. Granger, their mouths open in surprise!

"Come along, the bus will be waiting," she said.

"We're leaving already?" Brian asked, astonished.

"Hmmm . . . ," she said as her eyes narrowed at the both of them. "I hope you've learned enough about the Metis to describe one thing that was unique about their way of life. You spent far too much time in that exhibit," she said as she turned and followed her students to the museum's exit.

Brian turned to follow, but felt a roughness beneath his fingers.

"Hey, there's something scratched into the wood," he said, looking closely at the back of the cart.

Both boys leaned forward for a closer look.

D u m o n t

"Isn't that your name?" Dave whispered. "You don't think all that was real, do you?"

After a few seconds of thought, Brian said, "Naww . . .it was a virtual tour."

"It's about time museums were more kid friendly," he said, frowning slightly while looking back at the cart as they walked away.

"Then why does my whole body ache?" Dave asked as they were leaving the building.

"Mine too," Brian said, rubbing his rifle-bruised shoulder.

On that thought, both boys paused and turned to look back.

Standing at the door of the museum were John, Mary, Josh and Eleanor, smiling and waving.

"Must be one of those projection cameras used as a part of their virtual tours," Brian said, puzzled. "They probably have one for every exhibit."

"Yeah? Then why do they seem to be looking at us?" Dave asked.

"It is kind of spooky," Brian said as a thought occurred to him. "Hey, maybe we should come back to see the dinosaur exhibit? Imagine what that would be like!"

"I'll have to think about that one," Dave replied sarcastically as they boarded the bus. "I shudder to think what you might touch next."

"One thing for sure," Brian said. "I'll never say museums are boring ever again!"

STEPS IN TIME

"I WON'T DO IT," MELISSA SAID ANGRILY. "YOU can't make me."

"Melissa, honey," her mom said. "It's been a tradition that someone in our family participates in the Metis Assembly at least once every few years.

"Your father can't because of his leg," she said patiently. "And your brother needs to stay home to do your father's work."

"I'm not interested, and besides, I can't. It's just not in me," she said, spreading her arms wide.

"Kids my age are learning how to dance to hip hop music, not jig the *broom dance*," she said sarcastically.

"Can you imagine what the kids at school would say if they found out that I was jigging?" she said with eyes wide in horror.

"Think about it," her mom said gently. "Think of our family and the small part we've always played in celebrating a part of our culture."

With those words still ringing in her ears, Melissa walked out the door, fuming that her family would try to place a guilt trip on her. She had absolutely no interest in either jigging or attending any type of cultural event.

Well, that wasn't exactly true. Melissa would never admit the real reason to anyone. Many past fumbling attempts at jigging had proved disastrous. It always ended up being a waste of time and an activity that ended in frustration.

Glancing towards her great-grandmother's tamarack log cabin, Melissa decided to cool down before facing her family's disappointed looks.

For some reason, every generation of their family had spent time maintaining various parts of this particular home. Melissa could remember her grandfather carefully sanding, staining and waterproofing the outside logs. Over the years he had also stripped, stained and varnished a few household pieces.

It had something to do with the cabin being priceless. Mom and dad had spent time on the house, too. Dad had stripped and stained the floorboards and doors while mom had whitewashed the walls inside the cabin. The log cabin seemed to mean many things to different members of her family as it had with past generations.

Regardless, to 12-year-old Melissa, it was a place of refuge.

Melissa's dad, however, often jokingly referred to it as his doghouse.

Melissa stood at the door to allow her eyes to adjust to the dim interior of a house with no electricity. It was a practical home with two bedrooms, a curtained bathroom for privacy and an open area for the kitchen and living room. The design had something to do with making the most of the heat and light they could get naturally.

Mom had said that grandma would use a piece of string set in animal fat. When lit, this was their source of light in the evenings.

Melissa's favorite place was the cushioned couch near the stone fireplace, where she spent many hours. She walked with purpose towards the couch and closed her eyes as she laid her head on one of the down-filled cushions. She opened them briefly to give some serious thought to her mother's words.

There on the wall stood a beautiful lady dressed in a white-fringed dress. The lady was staring at her feet and stumbling about on the floor. Or so it seemed . . . .

"Melissa, a phone call for you," her brother Todd shouted from the house.

"Geesh, I must have dozed off," she muttered, blinking her eyes as she jumped up and ran to answer the phone.

"Hey Melissa, guess what?" Amy said, sounding excited. "I've been asked to perform at the Metis Assembly next month!"

"Doing what?" Melissa almost shouted.

"Square dancing!" Amy said. "Of course, I'd have to learn, but I wondered if you'd be interested in learning with me.

"I think it'll be a lot more fun if we learn together!" Amy suggested hopefully.

"My mom is trying to hook me into jigging and now you're seriously thinking of square dancing?" Melissa said in frustration. "Whatever next . . . the waltz?"

"Jigging?" Amy asked, ignoring Melissa's reaction.

"Yeah . . . my family laid it on pretty heavy," Melissa replied seriously. "I'm more interested in modern dances like hip hop or breakdancing."

"Well, I think I'll stick to the square dancing for now," Amy said slowly, but with purpose.

Melissa could hear the disappointment.

"Yeah, well . . . I'll think about it," Melissa sighed as she hung up the phone and walked back to the cabin.

She paused at the door to stare at the wall where the clumsy lady had appeared.

This time, however, instead of closing and opening her eyes, she simply closed them and refused to open them for any reason.

As soon as she closed her eyes, however, the lady in white appeared with her back turned to Melissa. She was standing in front of the fireplace, using her fingers to pull one of the stones loose. Finally, after much fingernail scratching and tugging, the stone pulled free from the wall. Melissa could see that the stone looked like it had been sliced to serve another purpose.

The lady carefully placed the stone on the floor and quickly placed a package in the hole that the stone had covered.

"Melissa, lunch is being served!" her mom shouted.

Melissa opened her eyes and focused on the fireplace, searching for the stone that she had seen in her dream.

Instead of rushing to the house, she felt drawn to the stone, and began scratching and tugging at its outer edges. Unbelievably, it moved slightly, and after more tugging broke free.

"Melissa, your lunch is getting cold . . . come on!" her mom called again.

"In a minute, mom!" Melissa shouted back.

Melissa carefully placed the stone on the floor and confidently reached into the hole for the package she felt certain was there.

"Wow!" she whispered in wonder as she held a package wrapped with what looked like the stuff used to make moccasins.

"Melissa, don't make me come out there!" her mother shouted again.

"Be right there!" she yelled back as she quickly placed the stone back in the wall and hid the package under the cushions.

Melissa waited until everyone was busy passing plates of sandwiches, fruits and vegetables.

She said quietly, "I had a dream about a beautiful lady dressed in a white-fringed dress. It was a strange dream because all I had to do was close my eyes and she appeared. Stranger yet is that I felt no fear. She showed me where a package had been hidden in the stone fireplace. Did such a lady live in our cabin?"

Dad dropped the plate of sandwiches while mom choked on a celery stick. Her brother Todd merely looked up, interested at the question and their parents' reaction.

"Well . . . that was quite a dream, Melissa," her mom replied, clearing her throat. "Considering you were only out there for a half hour."

"I don't think it was a dream," Melissa continued. "The first time I saw the lady, she was fumbling about with her feet. I just wondered if she had anything to do with the cabin and our family."

"Well . . . there were numerous stories about certain members of our family," her mom said vaguely. "Long ago, reading and writing were luxuries in a time when it was more important to prepare food and sew warm clothing for winter survival. Pen and paper supplies were in short supply and considered an unnecessary expense, so as stories were told and retold, they often changed with each storyteller.

"I was always fascinated with one story, however, although I'm sure that it like many others had changed over time as well.

"This story seems to match your dream. It goes like this . . . ," her mother began.

· · · ·

"Long ago, during the time of the beaver, there lived a chief's daughter of exceptional beauty and spirit. Everyone who saw Minawa loved her instantly. It was believed that her beauty combined with her spirit was a gift from the great Manitou. From the time of her birth, her tribe prospered, the people were content and life was good. Unfortunately, Minawa's mother had died during childbirth and so she was left to her aunt Keesha, who was a great medicine woman. Keesha loved her niece dearly and taught her the healing powers of plants so that Minawa might one day take her place as medicine woman.

"One day a Scottish trader named James visited their village and offered to trade supplies: brass and copper ornaments, cloth, needles and beads for beaver pelts and pemmican.

"However, when James saw Minawa, he fell instantly in love and instead of trading his supplies, he offered everything he had to marry Minawa. The chief was angry with the trader and sent him away.

"It would have been considered an insult to give a gift from Manitou for things that had no real value for his people.

"Weeks passed before the trader returned with even more supplies: knives, axes, blankets and a herd of 10 horses. The chief felt that this was a trade worth serious thought. The horses, combined with the supplies, would benefit his people, but could they trade Minawa and risk losing the spiritual gifts they owed to her presence? Would the great Manitou punish them for their greed?

"The chief decided to hold a council with his people and leave the decision to them. Keesha stepped forward during the assembly, angry that the chief would leave a decision such as this to the people.

"'Why not let Minawa decide for herself,'" she said to the assembly.

"'Spiritual gifts can't be traded,'" she stated firmly.

"Keesha told the people that she had prayed to Manitou and was shown a vision. To trade Minawa like an animal was unforgivable. The decision must be Minawa's.

"When James was brought forward amongst the council, he spoke of respecting, honouring and loving Minawa forever as his wife. Minawa saw into the heart of the trader, could hear the truth of his words and so agreed to marry him.

"The Chief, Keesha and the people were greatly saddened by the loss of Minawa. Keesha had always considered her niece as a daughter and so organized the women to sew a wedding dress. The dress was made using white leather with fringes sewn down into a V to her waistline, with a matching hemline and wraparound moccasins. As it was their custom, a gift of acceptance into the family was given to James. He honoured the gift by wearing his wraparound moccasins during the wedding ceremony. Keesha then prayed for a spirit of protection to be placed on Minawa's home and family. Keesha had loved her niece so dearly and mourned the loss of Minawa's presence that it is said her prayer moved the great Manitou.

"According to the story, Manitou promised Keesha that his spirit would always guide and protect Minawa and see to the spiritual needs of her children and descendants. The tribe would continue to prosper because they had allowed Minawa to choose.

"Minawa was married amongst her people and wore the wedding dress proudly. When it was time to dance, she joined the circle of dancers, as was their tradition.

"The Scotsman, however, carefully removed two pieces of shiny wood with strings from a case, rubbed them together and began to dance in a strange way to screeching music. The people were shocked as he stopped and then extended his hand to Minawa. Uncertain of what to do, Minawa bowed her head and prayed. How could she dance to honour both her people and her husband? Once again, James began to play the music made from wood.

"The spirit answered and guided her feet, stepping in time to the fiddle music in a circle dance that she loved yet following that of her husband's Scottish fiddle tune.

"Through time the jig has been danced in celebrations according to the jiggers' cultural background, whether English, Scottish or French Metis."

· · · ·

"Melissa, our great-grandmother was Minawa. Since the time of Minawa, the Metis people always believed that being Metis is about choice. The nation that was born from Minawa's choice along with many other men and women who made those same choices was the Metis Nation. According to historical fact, the children from these mixed marriages were called half-breeds, country born or Bois-Brûlés. The word Metis is accepted today to describe all descendants from native and European men and women from all cultural backgrounds. Some people decide to follow just one of their parents' cultures. In choosing to be Metis, you honour both. Of course, it's just a story," Melissa's mom finished.

After a moment of silence and thought, Melissa's mom continued. "Following the native way, the Metis have always held assemblies to discuss important issues that relate to our membership. As a part of this we encourage and promote celebrations of our culture. This is why our family has always played a small part in these celebrations. Like Minawa, it is now up to you to choose.

"Whatever you decide to do, Melissa, will be OK with us," Mom said gently.

"Well . . . I don't need a spirit to teach me how to jig," Melissa said, remembering the fumbling lady. "I need a friend."

. . . .

After lunch, Melissa phoned Amy.

"S'up?" Amy asked cautiously.

"I've decided to jig at the Metis assembly, but I need someone to help me learn," Melissa said. "Maybe we can help one another. I have a place where we can practice both of our dances in privacy."

"Cool!" Amy said, excited. "I have copies of the square dancing tapes that we use in our practices, and if I remember, one of the tapes has the Red River Jig."

With Amy due to arrive soon, Melissa searched the house for a cassette recorder and batteries. She then walked back towards the cabin to look through the package and its contents. The white-fringed dress and wrap-around moccasins were exactly as she remembered from her dream. Along with the dress, however, was a pair of moccasins made for a man. Melissa wrapped the items the way she had found them and placed them back in the stone wall.

. . . .

The girls practised every day for the entire month, and as rumour spread, other square dancers, jiggers and fiddlers soon joined them.

Finally, the day of the Metis Assembly arrived. Melissa had no idea what to expect or how many people would attend.

When the girls stepped into the hall, they were shocked to see that the hall was packed with people. There were square dancers of all ages grouped from young to old by their costumes. The girls in Amy's square dancing group were wearing a slanted eight symbol on their blue dresses while the boys wore multicoloured cloth belts.

Young children barely able to walk were either stepping or jumping up and down, dancing to the fiddling music. Each performance followed, one after the other in singing, square dancing and jigging, when Melissa heard her name announced.

"I can't do this on my own," Melissa whispered nervously as she pulled on the moccasins that matched the dress she wore from great-grandmother's package. To everyone who looked at the young girl dressed in the white-fringed dress, it looked as if Melissa were talking to herself.

"Help me," she prayed silently as the fiddle player began to bow the first few chords to prepare the jigger.

All the practising that she had done had not prepared her to face an audience of hundreds of people.

Then a strange thing happened. She *felt* more than *heard* the fiddler strumming the first few chords of the Red River Jig. The fiddler repeated them again, noticing her hesitation.

"I will guide you," the spirit whispered.

Melissa shuffled her feet, remembering the steps that she had seen in the vision from her great-grandmother.

Melissa stopped resisting and let her feet, body and spirit move to the music. Soon, she felt herself propelled forward, jigging and dancing in a circle, floating above the floor as the spirit overwhelmed her.

The crowd cheered and clapped as Melissa left the stage area.

She went to sit beside her mom and dad and discovered that she actually enjoyed watching the other performers.

When Amy's square dancing performance was over she quickly joined them.

"You were wonderful!" she said in disbelief. "It looked as if you were floating above the floor."

. . . .

The day passed too quickly and after a meal of bannock and moose stew, Melissa and her family headed home.

On their arrival, Melissa's mom went straight to the cabin and returned to the house with the leather-wrapped package.

She laid it carefully on the table, placing the man's moccasins to one side. Then she slipped her hand into a flap on the side of the hide. It was lined with a hard, shiny type of skin.

"I too found this package when I needed it," she said as she pulled out some papers. "Our great-grandmother, Minawa hid it in the fireplace. I'm not sure why she did such a thing. Maybe she felt that Manitou's spirit would stay close to her most prized possessions. Finding it would be proof of her legacy for each generation to help fulfill their spiritual or cultural needs. I also found a letter that she wrote, as well as a pencil sketch. This would be the only picture that we have. It's amazing that this stuff lasted this long."

Melissa gazed at the pencil sketch in awe. It was the lady that she had seen in her vision.

"I'll leave you to read her letter," her mom said. "It contains a message that I'm sure has fascinated our family for many generations and will continue to do so."

Melissa sat down and began to read.

"Life is filled with choices. My legacy to you is that you respect yourself, your family, your friends and the choices that you make. I leave this cabin and all my earthly possessions in the safekeeping of Manitou's spirit that he may fulfill his promise to help and guide you to fulfill all your spiritual and cultural needs . . . to infinity."

Melissa held the letter for a moment, smiled, and for the first time felt pride in being a Metis.

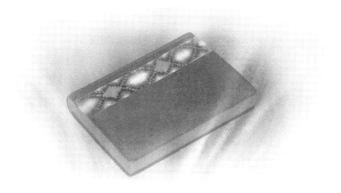

BETWEEN TWO WORLDS

TONY AND TEDDY HAD NEVER LEFT THE CITY before, so going on a wilderness vacation was a new experience. They had left their home and city of skyscrapers and shopping malls days ago, driving through a number of smaller towns that had grown fewer and farther apart. The boys had enjoyed themselves tremendously, fascinated by the changing scenery. The monotony, however, was taking its toll on 10-year-old Teddy as they traveled on a seemingly endless asphalt highway bordered by tamarack and spruce trees.

"How far do we still have to travel before we get to this resort?" he asked.

"According to the map, and the instructions I have from the owner, we should almost be there," his dad said. "And it's not a resort; it's a cabin in the bush."

"Are we really going to be there all alone?" Tony asked, a bit worried.

"I wouldn't say alone," Dad said, smiling. "Our closest neighbour lives five kilometres away, but I'm told that there's a radio if we should have any questions or run into any trouble. Don't worry, boys, I have instructions for that, too!

"I'd like to remind the both of you that I grew up in the north," Dad explained. "The living conditions were very much like where we'll be staying."

"Can we pack up and go home if we get bored?" Teddy asked.

"Uh . . . No! That would end up being about 24 hours after we arrive," Dad replied, a bit impatiently.

"Listen guys, I had enough extra money to pay for the rent on this cabin for one month," he said. "When I rented the cabin, it was the distance from the nearest town that made it the perfect place to get away from our *unwanted visitors*.

"I'm determined that this is going to be a great summer holiday for you and an inspiring one for me to hopefully write another book," Dad said.

The boys glanced at one another briefly. They knew from their Dad's tone of voice that there would be no changing his mind.

The next few hours were spent in silence as the boys looked out the windows, searching the forest and occasionally spotting birds and animals.

"There's the turn," Dad said suddenly, pointing toward a graveled highway.

"This road leads up into that mountain," he said as he turned. "Our cabin, however, is near a river that runs alongside the mountain."

The boys looked at one another with thankful expressions of similar thoughts. A wilderness vacation in the bush was one thing; a mountain was another.

"Look for a cabin, guys," Dad said. "According to my instructions, it's supposed to be a few kilometres from the main highway."

Some time had passed with still no cabin in sight.

Tony asked, "Is there such a thing as being too remote?"

"Is that it?" Teddy asked, squinting and pointing to a speck of gray amongst the green.

"Must be. It definitely has the look of cabins I've seen in history books," Tony answered as the cabin came painfully into sight.

"Come on boys, give it a chance," Dad said with a touch of humour.

"Did you say there was a river?" Teddy asked, excited. "Maybe it's shallow like those streams where the salmon swim and we'll be able to see some fish? Maybe we can even go fishing?"

Dad parked the van in front of the log cabin.

Seeing a spark of interest, he said, "You know what? You've been such good sports, I'll unload the van. I'd like to check the cabin out, get a fire going and unpack. There's a ball of yellow twine under your seat, Teddy. Why don't you boys go and see if you can find the river."

Teddy found the twine quickly and held it up, puzzled.

"The river is not very far," Dad said, checking his map and pointing them in the right direction.

"Tie a piece of that yellow rope around every sixth or 10th tree so that you can find your way back to the cabin. This is a huge forest and it would be easy to get lost. If you can do that, you can go on your own. I'll check up on you as soon as I'm done," he told the boys.

"Sure," Tony said, nodding in agreement. "I'll watch Teddy and we'll be careful."

As Teddy walked ahead, Tony followed his dad's instructions by stopping, cutting and tying a yellow rope around certain trees.

"Hey, I think I can hear water," Teddy shouted and broke into a run."

Teddy!" Tony yelled as he was tying off another rope. "Stay close, dad said it's easy to get lost."

When he turned to follow, Teddy was nowhere in sight.

"Teddy!" he yelled again.

"Owwwwww!" Teddy responded with a groan.

"Where are you?" Tony shouted urgently. "Keep talking so I can find you."

Following Teddy's voice, Tony found him lying on the ground, cradling his knee.

"You okay?" Tony asked, concerned as he checked his brother's injury.

"I tripped on something," Teddy replied. "I really banged my knee hard on it, too."

"Just a bad scrape, but look at your pants," Tony said. "I don't think dad's gonna be impressed."

"Well . . . accidents happen, even out here in the bush," Teddy mumbled.

"You must have tripped over a root or a branch," Tony said, looking around. "Can you bend your knee?"

"It bends, so I guess it's okay," Teddy said, getting up and scuffing the ground with his foot. "I tripped over something bigger than a root because my knee banged against it.

"See?" Teddy said as he limped over to reveal two pieces of wood half covered by branches that formed a giant X.

"Weird," Tony said slowly. "Doesn't X usually mark the spot?"

Teddy's eyes grew big and round.

"Treasure!" he said, and then seriously began digging and clawing through leaves and dirt with his hands.

"I wouldn't do that," a voice said. "You might not like what you find."

Startled, the boys looked up.

A man dressed in a fringed buckskin jacket with matching pants and mukluks stood before them. The strange outfit seemed stranger still when the man was wearing a fur hat in the summer.

The boys frowned.

"You must be the neighbour," Tony said.

"No. I'll be what you dig up if you keep digging," the man said, laughing.

"EEeewww!" Teddy stopped digging in disgust. "No treasure?"

"No treasure," the man replied, shaking his head sadly.

"Ghhosstt?" Teddy asked slowly as realization replaced disgust.

"I prefer to think of it as a presence with a purpose," he replied, smiling cheerfully.

"Awww . . . Teddy, you're such a ghost magnet," Tony said, now disgusted too. "So much for a wilderness getaway free from *unwanted visitors*."

"I can't help it," Teddy replied, shrugging his shoulders. "What are the odds of tripping over one out here?"

"There are others like myself?" the ghost asked, surprised.

The boys exchanged resigned looks.

"Try living in a city full of them," Tony replied. "Since Mom died, Teddy sees them all the time. My dad and I can only see them when Teddy's around."

"That must be awful," the ghost said in sympathy.

"It's amazing how many people forgot to say something or want something done *after* they've died," Tony explained.

"If you're really a ghost, then how old are you in ghost years?" Teddy asked, curious.

"Old enough to be tired of waiting for someone to stumble across my resting place," the ghost replied, "and old enough to be grateful, although I was only 21 years old when I died in the year of 1675."

"Wow! That makes you the oldest ghost we've ever met. Why did you die so far away from everyone?" Tony then asked suspiciously. "Did you do something bad? Were you mean, greedy, miserable or just plain evil?"

"You can't be that bad because I'm not afraid of you," Teddy said, smiling to show his support.

"Please tell me that you're the only one out here?" Tony asked. "If we can help you quickly, we might be able to save our vacation and still try to have a good time!"

"Shouldn't we get dad?" Teddy asked. "He was looking for an idea for his next book."

Tony sighed, ignoring his brother. "We normally start with the questions. Why are you still here? Or is there anything we can do?"

After centuries of lonely silence, the ghost was eager to begin his story.

"Well, I was never a mean-hearted person," he explained for Tony's benefit. "I died in a time when there weren't many people living in this area."

"Huh!" Tony snorted. "Look around, that's still true today!"

"The name my father gave me is Etienne. My mother named me Papishkon," he said, deciding to ignore Tony's rudeness. "I've been waiting centuries for someone to find me and hopefully to help me."

"Boys!" Dad shouted in the distance.

"We're here!" Tony shouted back.

"It's starting to get dark," Dad responded. "You better come in now. Just leave the yellow strings on the trees."

"Be right there!" Teddy yelled.

"I need you to get a bag of gold," the ghost said urgently.

"I just knew there had to be treasure," Teddy said cheerfully.

"Well what do you know," Tony said, surprised. "X really does mark the spot!"

"The X that you're so fascinated with is actually the cross of my canoe paddles," the ghost said patiently. "I stuck them in the ground to mark my resting place. There's nothing special about them other than they tripped you."

"So if the gold is not buried with you, then where is it?" Teddy asked.

"Not far, just follow me," he said. "You might want to keep on tying your rope on the trees, though."

True to his word, they hadn't walked far when they heard the river roaring nearby.

"I left the gold in a cave," he said, pointing to a mound at the base of the mountain. "Once you clear away the branches and leaves, you should find the entrance."

The boys began to scratch and pull at dead branches and leaves until they uncovered a hole. They looked at one another with disbelief and exchanged a silent, *I'm not going in there*, look.

"I'll go," Teddy volunteered. "I'm smaller, and after all this time the walls may collapse."

"Better yet, I'll tie this rope around your waist and leg . . . just in case you get in a tight spot," Tony said.

The entrance to the cave had narrowed with the passing of time. Teddy had to crawl on his grazed knee to get through. Tony could judge his brother's progress by the "Ow, ow, ow" muttering.

Tony could see streaks of light from his key chain flashlight. When Dad bought the mini-flashlights for both of them, he had jokingly explained their importance in using the outdoor facilities. Tony was grateful that they had found another use.

"See anything?" Tony asked.

"Yeah," Teddy said, amazed, squinting at the dim lighting from his flashlight. "There really is a cave!"

"There you are," Tony heard Teddy say, surprised. "I wondered if you would come in here, too."

The ghost had apparently followed him.

Minutes went by when Teddy yelled, "I found it...the bag of gold! Hey, there's even a canoe in here. How did you get that canoe in here?"

After some mumbling, Teddy yelled, "Coming out!"

When Teddy's head peeked through the hole, Tony couldn't help but laugh. "You look like a mole!"

Forgotten was the fear of going into the hole, replaced by relief at having made it out alive. Teddy smiled to show his relief.

"Do you think it's real gold?" Teddy asked, shaking the bag.

"Let's take a look," Tony said.

With the bag opened the boys gazed at the shiny nuggets.

"Now what?" they said together.

"I want something done," the ghost said. "If you don't, my spirit won't rest and I'll be with you for the rest of your lives."

"See?" Tony said, elbowing his brother. "They always want something *said* or *done.*"

"Well, I think it would be cool to have your very own ghost," Teddy said, clutching the bag of gold tightly to his chest. "We can keep him around, find out what he can and can't do, have lots of fun and be rich, too."

Tony looked at his younger brother in frustration and said, "You know sometimes I think you need to give your head a shake."

For a 12-year-old boy, Tony was remarkably sensible.

"The reason we're out here is to get away from *his kind*," Tony said. "And no amount of gold is going to buy us peace and quiet."

"So what did you intend to do with this gold before you died?" Tony turned and asked the ghost.

Surprised that his death was mentioned in such a matter-of-fact way, the ghost continued with his story.

· · · ·

"Well . . . as I mentioned before, my name is Etienne, but please call me Papishkon. I've been roaming this area for over 200 years.

"My father, who was French, sent me to be educated in France when I was 10 years old. It's sort of ironic and sad at the same time because my mother and her family, who were native, taught me how to survive in the wilderness. The school in France taught me how to read, write and work with numbers, but when I returned to Canada, I felt compelled to return to the wilderness. My father was angry, of course.

"He hoped that I would work at one of the fur-trading posts that were being established as the voyageurs began to explore the western regions of Canada.

"With my brown hair and fair skin, I could easily pass for a Frenchman. My father insisted that I could play an important part in establishing a trading post for France.

"But I wasn't sure what I wanted to do with my life. So, I joined the voyageurs and traveled the rivers and waterways. It was along this river that I first spotted the gold. I worked and waited until I had saved enough money to outfit myself as an independent trapper. My family supported this because they felt that I was headed in the right direction.

"My mother worked hard at home, but she would still take time to visit her people. The women worked hard, processed the furs and actually kept the fur trade alive with their hard work. It was my mother who taught me how to prepare the beaver skins for drying.

"I came here, spent the winter trapping beaver and in the spring went home and sold three bundles of furs. I bought more supplies to last me through the summer and returned here to pan for the gold. Before I left home, my parents gave me a special gift.

"I spent many evenings thinking about what I was going to do with the gold. Finding the gold brought choices and I was torn between two worlds.

"I could deny who my parents were, forget my home and family, return to France and live the rest of my life a wealthy man. Or, I could return home, establish my own fur-trading post and hire voyageurs to take my furs to Montreal.

"It wasn't until I lay sick that I realized that I owed my existence and my ability to survive in the wilderness to my parents – especially to my mother and her people."

Papishkon paused and pointed at the bag of gold. "There's a hand-stitched and beaded leather journal at the bottom of that bag of gold. My mother gave it to me before I left home. I recorded my thoughts and experiences in it daily along with dates and maps of places I traveled. I also drew a map to where I found the gold.

"I was going to ask that you place the journal beside my canoe paddles so that I have something of my mother beside me. Then I heard you mention that your dad is writing a book?"

"My dad's a writer," Tony said slowly. "His first published book earned some extra money. That's how we were able to come here for our first vacation ever."

"Here's a thought," Teddy said. "What if I take this bag of gold to my dad, show him your grave, your cave and your journal. If he's interested in your story, we'll give him the bag of gold to help pay for publishing and promoting the book."

"What do you think?" Teddy asked.

"It sounds like a good idea," Papishkon said thoughtfully. "I'll never get a chance to say I'm sorry to my family. They'll never know what happened to me and that I was coming home. But if your dad can tell my story, people will know what it was like to be a Metis in my time and maybe draw strength from my experience. I learned too late that it's not about money or gold. It's about accepting who you are, appreciating what you have and then deciding what to do with your life."

"I'm curious. How did you die?" Teddy asked. "All your stuff is still in the cave."

"I should have realized that the cave was actually a bear's den," Papishkon said. "She came home to hibernate, I got mauled and my wounds became infected. The infection brought a fever so that I couldn't treat myself. With no one to bury me, I marked my resting place with my canoe paddles. The last thing I remember is wishing that I had my journal."

In silence, the boys walked back to the cabin to see what was to be done with their companion, the journal and the bag of gold.

"I better prepare Dad for this one," Teddy said with a backward glance.

"Dad!" he yelled as they approached the cabin. "Remember when you said that this was the ideal place to get away from those *unwanted visitors?*"

They could hear a scuffling of running feet.

"No!" Dad responded immediately, throwing open the cabin door.

Seeing Papishkon, Dad groaned. "Did you hitch a ride or just follow us? Not that it makes any difference. I'd just like to know where we went wrong in our plans."

Papishkon shrugged his shoulders and looked confused.

"I was always here," he said.

"Impossible!" Dad retorted. "No one has ever lived here except my wife's family."

"What?" Tony and Teddy shouted together in disbelief.

Dad paused briefly then glanced away with a heavy sigh. "I didn't want to tell you this earlier, but the cabin once belonged to your grandparents," he said.

"Your mother sold the cabin and moved to the city after her grandparents died," Dad explained. "She used the money to put herself through college. That's where I met her. After she passed away, I found a copy of the bill of sale for the cabin. Everything just seemed to fall into place to make this vacation possible. I hoped that by bringing you here, you would appreciate how she grew up and somehow it might help us deal with her death."

"Pardon me," Papishkon said. "Did I hear you say that your wife's family had always lived here?"

"Yes," Dad responded. "She said that the cabin belonged to their family as far back as her grandparents could remember."

Seeing the shocked effect that the mention of their mother had on the boys, he then continued his explanation.

"Your mother often talked about this place and her childhood. She hoped that some day we would be able to afford to buy it back. Living in a city was just too expensive for that to be possible. We both hoped that at the very least, we would one day be able to afford to take you guys on a wilderness vacation. She would have loved to be here right now teaching the both of you how to survive in the wilderness. You see, your mother was Metis."

"Hey," Teddy said, slowly remembering the story. "Papishkon's a Metis."

"Was her name Elizabeth?" Papishkon asked.

"Yes!" everyone shouted expectantly.

"Is she here?" Teddy asked. "Why can't I see her?"

"I remember the families, but I haven't seen Elizabeth in a long time," Papishkon said apologetically.

The boys glanced down. She was the one ghost they would have loved to see.

"Well," Dad said, breaking the thoughtful silence. "We're here now and maybe mom knows we're here, too."

"Dad?" Teddy asked. "Papishkon has a story to tell. It sounds like that inspiration you were looking for, for your next book."

Dad merely nodded his head.

• • • •

The day quickly passed into evening as Papishkon told a fascinating story of exploring new lands and a way of life long forgotten.

"Look, Papishkon's journal and his bag of gold," Teddy said, showing his Dad at the conclusion of the story. "He said we could have it if we help him."

Dad seemed more fascinated with the journal than with the gold.

"Papishkon," Dad said, turning a few pages. "I hate to admit it, but we're going to need you to stick around for awhile.

"Your journal is written in French," he explained as he held the journal up for the boys to see.

"As for the gold, we'll set some of the money aside for your education," Dad told the boys. "I'm not sure about the rest. We can discuss that later."

• • • •

The boys spent the rest of the month learning outdoor survival skills with Papishkon.

The first thing that Papishkon felt that they needed to know was how to make a fire without matches.

"The bark from the birch tree is like paper. You peel the bark off, place small dry twigs on top of the bark. Find two larger dry sticks. Lay one of the large sticks on top of the twigs. You can pile little strips of bark around that stick. Take the other stick, place it in the middle of the other stick and begin rolling it between your hands. The sticks rubbing together will heat up and cause the bark strips to burn," he explained as he demonstrated.

"If there are no birch trees around," he continued. "Use dry leaves or grass."

He then showed them how to catch fish without a hook and how to build a rabbit trap without wire.

Most importantly, Papishkon showed the boys how to find the four directions so they'd never get lost in the bush.

"Moss grows on the north side of the trees," he explained. "Or, if you're in an area of evergreen trees like spruce and pine, the north side will always have fewer branches."

During the evenings Papishkon would read aloud from his journal to dad, who listened and scribbled notes. While the boys spent their days with Papishkon, Dad spent his days writing feverishly.

On occasion, he would take a break and spend time with them as time allowed between cooking, cleaning and writing.

Days passed swiftly into weeks when the vacation came to a painful end. Papishkon became silent and moody as that day approached. They hadn't seen or heard from him at all on the day they had spent packing. With their supplies loaded and packed tightly in the van for the trip home, Dad and the boys visited Papishkon's grave to bid their farewells.

"Maybe he just couldn't bear saying goodbye," Teddy said, concerned as they walked back and climbed into the van.

As they traveled back to the city, Teddy said, "Dad, Papishkon suggested that we should use some of the gold to buy the cabin and the land that includes the cave."

"Hey, Teddy, didn't Papishkon mention that he drew a map in his journal showing where he found the gold?" Tony asked.

"Gosh!" Teddy exclaimed. "I was so upset, I forgot to leave the journal!"

The ghost sitting behind the boys merely smiled.

"Don't worry, boys," he said. "I've decided that this family needs me, at least for a little while."

The van came to a screeching halt.

"You have my journal," Papishkon reminded them, smiling at their shock. "Remember when I said that I needed something done?

"If you don't place my journal on my grave, my spirit won't rest and I'll be with you for the rest of your lives.

"Remember that?" he asked. "Well, I hoped you wouldn't, so I disappeared for a few days.

"Your mother visited me and asked if I would stay awhile," Papishkon said. "She'd like me to teach you boys more about what it's like to be Metis.

"Your mother believes we share something in common, Teddy," Papishkon explained. "She said that our grief has left us torn between two worlds. By helping you, I'll find peace in knowing that I passed along my mother's teachings. When you realize that your mother loved you and knew how you felt, you won't be troubled by ghosts anymore."

Teddy nodded knowingly and whispered back, "Thank you, Papishkon. I promise that if there ever comes a day that I can't see you anymore, I'll always remember your journal."

"Well, I need to get back to the cabin, so I'll be looking forward to your visit next summer," Papishkon said and disappeared.

Dad and the boys looked at one another and spent the next few hours in silence.

"The first thing we need to do when we get back to the city is take this gold to the bank and then buy that cabin," Dad said, interrupting their thoughts.

The rest of the trip was filled with plans for the gold and the book.

"I have a tentative title for the book," Dad said. "How does this sound: 'Papishkon: Man Between Two Worlds.'"

DANIEL'S CULTURAL ESSAY

"WE WILL BE CELEBRATING A NEW SCHOOL EVENT called Cultural Appreciation Week," Mrs. Porter announced to the class.

"I would like each of you to write an essay about one interesting person in your family or an event that depicts your cultural background," she said.

"This will be your weekend assignment. All essays are due next Friday, at which time, I will be asking each of you" – she paused briefly for effect – "to read your essay to the class."

"Local businesses have donated prize packages containing CD Walkmans, gift certificates, backpacks, movie passes and much more to support Cultural Appreciation Week. Each classroom will be awarding one of these prize packages to the student with the best written essay. I would like proper research done along with a bibliography," she finished, and then dismissed the class.

"What does depict mean?" Joe whispered to his friend Daniel as they gathered their homework.

"I don't know," Daniel said, scratching his head.

"I guess we'll have to check it out in the dictionary before we begin writing," Joe laughed jokingly.

"Do you have any ideas on what you're going to write about?" Daniel asked.

"I'll have to ask my Grandpa. The only thing I remember about our family is that they immigrated to Canada in 1917," Joe said.

"They must have brought some cultural stuff with them from Ukraine," Joe said. "What about you?"

"Hmmm . . . well, I'm not really sure about my family's background. It's all so mixed up!" Daniel said. "My mom is part Scottish mixed with native and my dad is part native but mixed with French. So . . . what does that make me?" Daniel asked.

"Pretty mixed up!" Joe laughed, waving as he got on the bus.

. . . .

As he slowly walked home, Daniel thought about what he could write for his essay. It would be nice to win that new CD Walkman! That wasn't going to happen if he couldn't find an interesting person or event in his family.

"It would be great to write about both," he thought when he remembered his grandparents were planning to visit that weekend.

Daniel decided that his research would have to begin with his grandparents. If he couldn't find anything interesting in his family then he'd have to do his research at the library on a French or Scottish event.

When his grandparents arrived later that afternoon, he walked out to greet them.

"Grandpa, I have to write an essay and I'm hoping you can help me," he pleaded.

"This essay must be really important if you can't give us a hug first," Grandma said, as she grabbed and kissed him.

"Can't promise anything until I hear more about this essay," Grandpa said, surprised.

"Well, my assignment is to write about an interesting person in my family or an event that depicts my cultural background," Daniel said.

"That's a pretty serious essay," Grandpa said as he hauled suitcases out of the trunk.

"Let me think about it while I'm resting and I'll try to have an answer after dinner tonight," he said, handing Daniel one of the suitcases.

. . . .

That evening when the dishes were cleared away Grandpa cleared his throat and said, "I think I have a story for your essay, Daniel.

"I can't believe that I forgot about this particular story," he said. "My grandparents told me when I was your age! As soon as I closed my eyes to rest, I thought of them and the story about my great-grandfather.

"If you hadn't asked me, I never would have thought to share it with you or your father," he continued.
"It would have been lost forever.

"This story is about your great-grandparents," he said, clearing his throat. "Although they were Metis, they were originally from the Caugnawaga Reserve near Montreal. They moved to the Prairie provinces with many family members to work as guides for settlers and explorers as well as to hunt the buffalo.

"The women were hard workers! Nothing was ever wasted!" Grandpa explained. "Whenever the men brought home buffalo, moose or deer meat, the women would begin processing it into pemmican.

"When each family had enough pemmican to last the winter, they would begin packing the extra supply in bags made from buffalo or moose skin and bury it the ground.

"I remember asking my grandmother this question:
'Why did they make so much pemmican?'
"'Maybe it will be a long winter,' she had said. 'Anyway, we should always have extra . . . just in case it's needed.'"

"Wait a minute," Daniel interrupted. "What's pemmican?"

"Pemmican was one of the most important foods that the native and Metis people made in order to survive," Grandpa explained. "The fur traders, the voyageurs and then the early settlers depended on pemmican for their survival, too. Making pemmican was a long process. Grandpa would bring home a buffalo or a moose. Grandma would cut the meat into long strips and then hang them out to dry in the sun or over a smoky fire.

"She would use her knife to cut strips into the meat as it was drying. When the meat was thoroughly dried, it became tough and hard so that it could be broken into little pieces. She would then place the dried pieces of meat along with some dried saskatoons or blueberries into a bowl or a bag and pound everything into a powder using a stone mallet. Then she would boil some animal fat and pour just enough into the powdered meat and berries to form pemmican cakes. When you looked at the size of the animal and the size of the pemmican it produced, you'd wonder how such a large animal could produce only a small amount of pemmican. The amazing thing about pemmican is that you'd never go hungry.

"Long ago, much of Canada was covered with bush, and most of the traveling was done on foot or by canoe following the waterways. Pemmican

was very filling and it was light to carry
when traveling.

"If you wanted a hot meal, you could break off
a chunk, throw it into a pot of water, and add wild
vegetables like onions, carrots or pine nuts, to
make a tasty stew called Rubaboo.

"Something that wasn't common knowledge
among the Europeans was how to store
pemmican so that it wouldn't spoil. The secret
was to place pemmican in a raw buffalo hide
and sew it up tightly with sinew.

"Pemmican could be buried in the ground for
two to three years and dug up ready to eat.

"But NOW . . . I can begin a reaallly interesting
story about your great-grandfather Louis
Delaronde, nicknamed Ouisa," Grandpa said.

Daniel listened carefully, writing notes on
important details as Grandpa shared his story.

· · · ·

Friday loomed over Daniel like a shadow, but he
kept busy writing and rewriting until he was
finally working on the final draft. He had done his
research and had taken the entire week to work
on the essay he titled *Daniel's Cultural Essay*.
After listening to Grandpa's story, the next
morning Daniel had gone to the public library. He
found books on native and Metis peoples and the
importance of pemmican. There was even a war
fought over it, which led to The Battle of Seven
Oaks in 1816! He found another book that

included the process of making pemmican. He searched through all of the books and found that Grandpa was right!

There was no mention of storing pemmican in a raw buffalo hide. Daniel noted his resources in a bibliography at the end of his essay.

. . . .

Early Friday morning, Daniel was ready, and listened with interest to each presenter while waiting his turn. Since he was the last one to hand in his essay, it looked like he would be the last one to read.

Joe began to read his essay. "It was due to the Bolshevik Revolution that my family immigrated to Canada in 1917. In their haste to flee Ukraine, they had to leave a lot of their valuable possessions.

"One item that my grandmother brought to Canada is an embroidered tablecloth that had been passed down from her grandmother . . . "

Daniel's name was called next. With a deep breath and shaking hands he began to read.

"According to my grandfather, my great-grandfather Louis Delaronde was a famous and respected Metis guide around the mid to late 1800s.

"Ouisa, as he was called, was originally from the Caugnawaga Reserve near Montreal.

"There were still parts of Canada that hadn't yet been explored and properly mapped. In his lifetime, he was hired to guide both settlers and explorers from Montreal to the Rocky Mountains. There was one story, however, that stood out from all the rest. It had been an especially hard winter with heavy snowfalls and food supplies were in demand.

"The Hudson's Bay Company had trading posts that provided settlers and trappers with a variety of supplies and food.

"However, they were situated long distances apart, and several days of traveling were needed in order to get from one trading post to another.

"On one of Ouisa's trips up north, he was carrying a load of much-needed supplies and pemmican for the Hudson's Bay Company when he was caught in a blizzard. The blizzard had been so severe and the snowfall so heavy that he got lost.

"Since there was no rising sun to give him directions on north, south, east or west, he wandered for several days looking for markers on the trees that he always set for himself.

"He knew that the pemmican would keep him alive, but he wouldn't eat it. One reason was that it didn't belong to him and the other was that it was badly needed at the outpost.

"Rather than eat the pemmican, Ouisa first chewed on his moccasin strings and then on the fringes from his leather coat. The bitter taste made him more alert and when mixed with snow became more chewable and filling.

"Finally, on the seventh day, he not only found one of his markers but also met some trappers who had been sent to look for him.

"The one aspect of this story that is culturally relevant is in the making and trading of pemmican by native and Metis people. Pemmican was made during the spring and fall in preparation for winter. The process of making pemmican was to mix dried powdered meat with saskatoons or blueberries and then add just enough melted fat to form a cake or ball. Pemmican was highly prized by fur traders, voyageurs and early settlers. They would trade items such as metal knives, pots, axes, blankets, beads and any other items that either native or Metis people found useful.

"Pemmican was very filling, nutritious, light to carry and wouldn't spoil. When traveling, a little pemmican would last a long time over great distances. Native and Metis people could afford to trade pemmican because they knew the secret of storing it so that it would last for years.

"The one interesting thing about my great-grandfather and many like him is that without his willingness to guide and teach the early settlers how to survive, many European people would have perished . . . possibly even your own ancestors."

The classroom was silent as students looked from Daniel to Mrs. Porter.

"Did you research your essay for factual information?" Mrs. Porter asked.

"Yes," Daniel replied. "I included a bibliography at the end of my essay. In researching books about pemmican and its importance in the early development of Canada, I discovered something interesting."

"What was that?" Mrs. Porter asked, leaning forward with interest.

"Long ago, people didn't have electricity and so there was no way to preserve food other than canning in jars. Native and Metis people knew how to store pemmican so that it would last for years," he said proudly.

"How many of you feel that Daniel's essay should be considered for the prize package?" Mrs. Porter asked, clearly impressed.

All arms shot up at once!

"Before you sit down Daniel," Mrs. Porter said, "what is more important? To win the prize package or to learn about your family and cultural background?"

Daniel thought for a moment.

"I really wanted the prize package and still do. But, by researching and writing the essay," he said thoughtfully, "I learned that I am Metis.

"I also learned that the Metis played an important part in Canadian history. Through my research, I discovered that we were sort of like a living bridge for our families and the people from other nations whatever their cultural backgrounds," Daniel said.

"One of the requirements for the prize package was a well-written essay and the other was to promote cultural awareness," Mrs. Porter said to the class.

"Congratulations, Daniel! You win the prize package," she announced as the class applauded.

THE VOYAGEUR'S SYMBOL

"THIS IS SO STUPID," PETE WHISPERED TO HIS best friend Jake as the school bus came to a stop in front of the art gallery.

"Yeah," Jake agreed reluctantly. "I think our teacher's an airhead."

Both boys turned to look at the object of their disgust.

Ms. Jenson was one of the prettiest and youngest teachers at their school. The grade six class had been excited when they heard that she was going to be their homeroom teacher.

The older and more experienced teachers had really bad reputations. They were organized, demanded punctuality in everything and gave lots of homework assignments. Ms. Jenson, however, had given lots of what she called *quizzes*. Everyone knew that they were really tests to see how much they knew and remembered from last year. The boys had hoped that this school year would be different from all the others.

"How can you learn anything about the fur trade just by looking at a bunch of paintings?" Jake asked as they got up to leave.

Pete voiced his support quietly. "Museums have more interesting things to see and do than art galleries. I can learn more from looking at pictures in history books. At least you can read the information that's placed around them."

"Oh well, the bright side is we're out of school for the day," Jake whispered as the class lined up to pass Ms. Jenson.

"You know ... there could be a bad side," Pete whispered back as a thought occurred to him.

They both paused briefly to look back at Ms. Jenson before walking up the steps to enter the gallery.

"Ms. Jenson might be one of those teachers who likes to play tricks on her students," Pete continued. "She would use the word *challenge*, but I smell an *assignment*. We could get hit with one of those *quizzes* when we get back to school tomorrow."

"Good thinking," Jake said, surprised at his friend Pete's logic.

"Maybe she's checking to see how much we'll *absorb* from the paintings." Pete chuckled at his own joke.

"It might not be a bad idea to take notes," Pete suggested.

"Notes on what?" Jake asked in disbelief.

Ms. Jenson had asked the class to assemble at the gallery's main entrance.

"OK, class," she spoke loudly, and then waited until she had everyone's attention. "We have a special guide who is a professional artist. He has offered to take us on a tour of the Fur Trade exhibit. At the end of the tour, he has invited us next door to an art studio where he will teach us step-by-step how to draw an object of our choice. I think that would be an exciting end to what I think will be an informative afternoon.

"Mr. Robert Lavelle has spent many years studying and painting historical people, places and things," she continued. "He can explain the process of how he does this and then what you need to look at specifically when viewing each of the paintings on display. I would like each of you to note the artist, the scenery, the actions and any other special details."

Pete smirked as he elbowed Jake at this last statement. Jake merely rolled his eyes while Pete dug in his shirt pocket for a notepad and pen.

Mr. Lavelle cleared his throat as he stepped forward.

"Right then," he said and then paused. "I think the best way to begin this tour is to introduce myself. As your teacher mentioned, my name is Robert Lavelle. I have been painting historical pictures for 23 years. As a result, I have spent many hours in libraries all over the world researching a number of civilizations – in particular, their history and culture. When we stop to discuss each of these pictures, I need you to guess the time in history that you think each painting was created.

"Let's focus on the first painting on display," he said as the class crowded around the object of his attention.

"This particular painting is very powerful in the messages we perceive from this one scene," he said, waving his hand artistically. "The artist has created a realistic image almost like a snapshot, including his subjects' actions, to show us how the voyageurs worked together in a canoe brigade."

"Artists must have their own ideas of beauty," Pete whispered to Jake. "Next, he'll be talking about depth."

"The use of paint is so deliberate, the effect is almost three-dimensional," Mr. Lavelle continued. "It leaves the perception that one can almost step into the painting. Long ago, and especially here in Canada during the fur trade era, it wasn't realistic to carry jars of paints, brushes and canvas. So, how do you think artists were able to create their paintings?"

The question was thrown out abruptly and hung in the air, as silent as its audience.

As usual, those students who had been daydreaming shook themselves alert while the few who had been listening responded.

"Memory?" one girl responded.

"Wouldn't it have been easier to carry a pad of paper and pencils?" Jake asked.

"Good answers," Mr. Lavelle applauded. "The artist would indeed carry a supply of paper and pencils. While traveling, if an area of land or a group of people were found to be inspiring, they would lightly pencil-sketch the scenes. Later on, when they returned home, they would have to rely heavily on memory when mixing paints for their pencil sketches.

"As you may or may not know, the fur trade existed largely due to the economics of supply and demand," he explained. "The demand for furs originated from European countries. The aboriginal people along with fur traders and the voyageurs supplied this demand. In this particular scene, please pay attention to the placement of the voyageurs. This was important. The man at the front is the avant or bowsman. He would set the paddle strokes and was the captain of the canoe. Notice that he carries a larger paddle for manoeuvring in rapids. There were anywhere from six to 14 middle paddlers, with a gouvernail or steersman at the stern of the canoe.

Voyageurs were employed by the Hudson's Bay or the North West Companies and sometimes by independent fur traders to transport furs from the interior of Canada to Fort William. They would use the rivers and lakes as their highways and *portage* their canoe along with supplies over land in order to connect to the next body of water. For hundreds of years, this was the primary method of travel in Canada.

"The next painting will show us the type of work each man was assigned when it was time to *portage*," he said, turning to lead the class to the next painting on exhibit. "We can actually see the physical labour each man experienced as they *portaged* over land."

Jake and Pete lagged behind as the rest of the class followed closely behind Mr. Lavelle.

"Why would anyone risk their life over animal skins?" Pete asked, leaning forward as something in the painting caught his eye.

He looked at Jake's neck and then at the painting again.

Following Pete's gaze, Jake leaned forward too. As his eyes attempted to focus on the painting his vision became blurred.

Jake blinked his eyes rapidly to clear them. When that failed, he squeezed them shut. Oddly, he could hear the sound of running water and then feel sprinkles of water on his face. Curious, he slowly opened one eye.

"Whoa!" he shouted in fear and surprise.

The man sitting next to him said, "Don't worry, we'll be on land shortly."

Startled, Jake jerked his body away, only to feel a body bumping him back.

He turned to the bump.

"Pete! Jake?" The names were shouted in unison and then carried by the wind. The boys sighed with relief at seeing one another, until they looked around and realized where they were.

"We're in a canoe!" Jake said in amazement.

"And the canoe's in the water," Pete said slowly, stating the obvious.

"This isn't possible!" Jake muttered to himself. "I must be dreaming. I'm probably still in bed. If I slap myself, maybe I'll wake up!"

Pete elbowed Jake's ribs, bringing him painfully back to reality.

"This looks like the painting in the art gallery," Pete suggested with shocked disbelief.

"That's impossible!" Jake squeaked back in a whisper. "Are you trying to suggest that we're somehow in a painting?"

"I don't know," Pete whispered back, worried. "It's the only thing that makes sense."

"How could this happen?" Jake asked.

"The better question is how do we get out?" Pete whispered back, worried. "What's the last thing you remember?"

"You were looking at the painting," Jake replied. "I wondered why, so I leaned forward to look and my eyes started to get blurry."

The canoe's abrupt shifting movements interrupted their conversation.

The water had become white and frothy as the stillness turned into a torrent of rushing water.

"Look, the avant is signaling," Jake said. "We must be coming to some rapids."

The canoe was indeed turning to face the rocky shore.

"The avant?" Pete asked. "What language are you speaking and how do you know what it means?"

"It's French and I was listening to Mr. Lavelle's presentation," Jake replied, watching their approach to shore.

When they were close to the shoreline, the paddlers seated ahead and directly behind the boys jumped out of the canoe and guided it closer to shore.

When all the paddlers were standing in the shallow water, the avant and the gouvernail stepped out of the canoe and began passing huge canvas-wrapped parcels. The man who had been sitting next to them watched the unloading in silence.

"The guy sitting next to us must be the bourgeois," Jake whispered.

The canoe was then pulled closer to shore, and the boys along with their seated companion stepped out of the canoe and waded to land.

"Bourgeois?" Pete asked, puzzled. "I definitely don't remember Mr. Lavelle mentioning a bourgeois."

"I must have read about it in history books," Jake replied, more interested in observing what was happening than listening to Pete.

With the canoe empty, four of the paddlers hoisted it out of the water and carried it to shore. At the same time, another man began to make a fire. The boys and their companion stood to the side and watched this flurry of activity in silence.

"Boy!" the cook yelled.

"Be a good lad and fill this with water," he said, waving a pot to Pete.

When Pete returned, the cook filled the pot with peas along with a chunk of meat. With the pot hoisted over the fire, the cook began to throw some flour and other ingredients into a bag. Mixing and then shaking the flour mixture into blackened pans, he added some water. He then spread this mixture outward until it filled each of the pans and placed them over the fire to cook, too.

"The cook is making what is called *gallet* or *bannock*," Jake whispered.

"What is *gallet* or *bannock*?" Pete whispered back. "Is it safe to eat?"

"It's a kind of bread," Jake responded patiently. "It's very delicious."

"I didn't know you were such a history buff," Pete said, surprised. "Just how many books have you read?"

Not expecting an answer, Pete then asked curiously, "What does a *bourgeois* do?"

"The bourgeois is the agent hired by the fur trade company. He is in charge of the expedition, and supervises the loading and unloading of the cargo," Jake said.

"How do you know all this stuff?" Pete asked, giving Jake a sharp look.

"I must have read about it somewhere," Jake replied with a bit of impatience.

Once they had eaten, the bourgeois spoke. "If you'd like to get your paper and pencils, the canoe along with the parcels would make an excellent picture. The company would appreciate knowing how well we care for its supplies."

Shocked, the boys looked at one another.

"Sure," Jake said, clearing his throat. "Pete, if you'd be so kind as to get me my drawing tools. I'll go and appraise the scene to get the best angle."

"What tools?" Pete whispered.

"Check the baggage that was thrown at us," Jake whispered back.

When Pete finally joined him, he desperately asked, "Now what? You don't know how to draw!"

"How do you know?" Jake said, smiling smugly. "Have you ever seen my artwork?"

Jake strutted around with purpose, sat on a large rock and with a flamboyant waving gesture put pencil to paper. Pete leaned forward, watching Jake's pencil strokes of lines and circles. Soon, however, a picture began to emerge, with the canoe turned on its side along with the parcels stacked beside it.

The bourgeois had quietly walked up behind Jake.

"Excellent!" he shouted, impressed. "Once everyone is done eating and repacking, I'd like you to sketch the voyageurs as they are preparing to portage."

"It would really freak me out if you knew what he meant by *portage*," Pete mumbled.

Jake ignored the comment and watched as the governail and the avant along with four others prepared to carry the canoe. He quickly sketched the scene. For once, Pete remained silent, content with watching the scenes created by Jake's pencil. It was when everyone was lining up to lift the canoe and prepare to carry the parcels that Jake tapped Pete with a light backhanded punch.

"Did you notice that everyone here is pretty much the same height?" he asked.

Not wishing to be outdone in note-taking, Pete responded, "Did you also notice that most of the voyageurs are young?"

"I don't remember this," Jake said, surprised at their discovery.

"What do you mean you don't remember this?" Pete whispered back. "How could you remember something that isn't even possible?"

Jake and Pete watched as the remaining voyageurs helped one another by taking turns placing parcels on their backs. During this process Pete noticed something dropping to the ground.

"That strap they're placing around their foreheads is called a tumpline," Jake explained. "The end of the tumpline is tied securely around a parcel. Once the parcel is secured on the voyageur's back, he will lean forward and another parcel will be placed on top of the previous package."

Pete looked at Jake as though he had grown two horns and a tail.

Jake decided to sketch this scene as well when he overheard a few of the men.

"Hoñhi lii katraveñ ji'liivr paké nawach ati kushikwanoh to lii zaañ," peyak eñ wayazheur ati itaapiw e'ati kanawaahpatak lii paké kiiyaapich chi naashtaachik.

"Eñ viyiu piikishkwewin anima," eñ nut wayazheur itwew. "Kiyaapich kika itwaan é'wii puunatushkéyan."

Jake laughed as he translated this conversation for Pete in English.

"These 90-pound parcels get heavier every year," one of the voyageurs said, laughing as he looked down at the remaining parcel that had yet to be placed.

"That's old age talking," another voyageur responded. "Next, you'll be talking about retiring."

"You know this language?" Pete whispered, ignoring the joke and the laughing men.

"It's Michif," Jake replied. "It's a mix of Cree and French. It was the language used so people could understand certain words from both languages and know what the other was trying to say."

Pete remained silent at this new revelation. How could Jake know how to translate a language used a long time ago?

They continued to watch as the backpackers began to walk. They broke into a slow jog.

Pete remembered the dropped item and went to retrieve it.

"Why are they running?" Jake asked the bourgeois.

"Running at a slow pace helps to lighten the load by taking the weight off your back," the bourgeois replied, surprised.

Jake was busy sketching the new scene of the voyageur backpackers as they ran past him when he noticed something unusual. All of the voyageurs wore identical neck chokers. As the canoe bearers jogged by, he saw the same symbol on the bow of the canoe. Then he realized that the symbol matched the one he wore around his neck. The artist in him noticed that one man with a light-tanned complexion was wearing a bandana around his head while another man with a darker-toned complexion with brown hair wore a sash around the waist.

"I thought they were Frenchmen?" Jake asked.

"Our guide is a Metis, and so are a few of the paddlers. But you should know that, being one yourself," the bourgeois said, looking strangely at Jake.

Jake blinked his eyes rapidly in shock and surprise. His vision began to blur and he grew dizzy. He quickly squeezed his eyes shut.

"Oh my gosh, Pete," he said. "I think I'm going to faint."

After a few seconds, Jake slowly opened his eyes and realized that he was back in the art gallery with Pete.

"Whoa!" he said loudly. "What just happened?"

"I don't care," Jake answered gratefully. "I'm just glad we're back."

The boys glanced around quickly to see if anyone had noticed their absence. Everyone was exactly where they had been. Ms. Jenson was looking at them with the same stern look.

"It's like we weren't even gone," Pete whispered as he leaned forward.

"I think it happened when I blinked my eyes," Jake said. "I don't understand. I've blinked my eyes before and nothing like this has ever happened. Do you think it has something to do with the paintings?"

"What were you squinting at before we were drawn into the picture?" Jake asked, trying to solve the puzzle.

"Look! See for yourself . . . just please don't blink your eyes," Pete said.

Jake – or someone who looked like Jake – was sitting in the middle of the canoe.

"At first, my attention was caught by the symbol on the bow of the canoe. But then I realized that I had seen that symbol around your neck, so I looked closer at the painting. That's when I saw you blinking and then – whoosh, we were there," Pete said.

"Hmmm," Jake said thoughtfully. "My grandfather gave this choker to me only a few days ago. He said that it had been passed down in our family for generations. It was considered a good luck symbol, but I didn't know it had any connection to the voyageurs or the Metis. What I find really strange is that it's connected to these paintings."

"Yeah, but what does all this have to do with me?" Pete asked. "Why did I get sucked in, too?"

Pete had been so occupied trying to make sense of what just happened that he hadn't noticed that the notepad and pencil that he had held in his hand had been replaced by something else. Curious, he slowly opened his hand and saw that it was one of the voyageur chokers! It had belonged to one of the voyageur backpackers.

"If what we experienced wasn't real then how did you get that?" Jake asked.

The boys were stunned into silence.

"Can anyone guess the time in history these paintings were created?" Mr. Lavelle asked.

Jake wasn't sure how he knew the answer.

"The year was 1810," Jake said loudly. "The reason I know this is because my great-grandfather was a Metis artist and mapmaker. These were his paintings."

After a few seconds of surprised silence, Mr. Lavelle agreed. "That would be just about the right time."

"Now, you're really freaking me out!" Pete whispered, his lips barely moving. *"Why did you say that?"*

"I don't know," Jake said, touching the choker. "I just know."

As Mr. Lavelle, Ms. Jenson and the class moved through each of the paintings on exhibit, they would pause, briefly glancing in Jake's direction before continuing to the next painting.

During these brief pauses, Jake would add details to Mr. Lavelle's discussion that he thought were important.

In one of the paintings of the voyageurs paddling down a river, Jake noted that it was the chanteur, or singer, who would lead the men in a song so they could paddle in time to the music.

As each painting was discussed, Jake discovered that each truly was a snapshot into the past. History was coming alive through memories not his own.

When they came to the painting of the voyageurs portaging with their parcels, Jake explained and demonstrated how they used a tumpline around their foreheads to transport the parcels of furs and goods.

"The voyageurs worked as a team in all things. They would help place the parcels, which each weighed approximately 90 pounds, on one another's backs," he explained. "They would run at a slow jog for many hours before stopping to rest. These paintings show the hard work that was done during the fur trade by the native, Metis and European peoples in the exploration and development of Canada."

Ms. Jenson and Mr. Lavelle exchanged looks at this statement.

"I give up asking how you know all this stuff," Pete said, shaking his head. "I am so confused and I think I have a headache."

Jake then remembered what the bourgeois had said about his being Metis. Although he was never told that his family was Metis, Jake was determined to find out what that meant and to do some research.

At the end of the tour, the class walked next door to the art studio where Mr. Lavelle had promised to teach them the basics of drawing.

"This field trip to the art gallery turned out to be OK," Pete said as they tagged along behind. "Despite the live-action history lesson, I actually enjoyed myself and learned a lot, too."

"Yeah," Jake admitted, still trying to make sense about the day's events. "Ms. Jenson might turn out to be OK."

"There is one thing that *really* puzzles me, though," Pete said as they entered the studio. "I can hardly wait to see if you can draw as well as you did back there while we were *sort of* in the *eye-blinking* painting."

"My family has always been artistic," Jake replied, smiling. "My pencil sketches are of people and things we see in the city because that's what I see every day. It would be a real challenge for me to draw something I had never seen before. So I really don't believe that it was me drawing those pictures. Most of my drawings could be called doodling. This is stretching it a bit, but I think it was my great-grandfather."

"Why do you say that?" Pete asked.

"How else would I know all that information unless I lived it?" Jake replied. "There were just too many details."

"OK," Pete replied, accepting Jake's explanation. "I can buy into that. So, how do you explain my bringing back the choker?"

Jake paused and then responded, "To prove that for a moment in time, we were really there."

. . . .

A few weeks had passed when Mr. Lavelle stopped to visit Ms. Jenson's classroom. After a few whispered comments, Jake and Pete were signaled to step into the hallway.

"Jake, I thought you would be interested in something I've discovered," Mr. Lavelle said. "I wanted to let you know that we hadn't gotten as far as carbon dating the paintings before they were placed on display. The results show that they were painted approximately in the time period you mentioned. I also discovered that it was your grandfather who loaned us the paintings. They were exceptional and so vivid in detail that we included them in the fur trade collection. The only stipulation that came with the paintings was that we offer a tour to interested classes from your school. Ms. Jenson's class was mentioned specifically.

"Did you know that your grandfather had loaned us the paintings for our exhibit?" he asked curiously.

"No," Jake replied, drawing everyone's eyes as he reached to touch the voyageur choker. "Actually, I had never seen them before. They must have been in his attic.

"He passed away a few weeks ago," he said, suddenly realizing the source of the vision.

"I'm very sorry for your loss," Mr. Lavelle said.

"This is probably not the best time, but I was impressed by the pictures you drew during my art class. You have a great eye for detail and a natural talent for bringing it out. It would be a shame to see that talent wasted. If you're interested, I hold classes on Tuesday and Thursday evenings. Ms. Jensen has agreed to inform interested students and parents with enrollment information. Hopefully we'll see you there."

"Thank you," Jake replied.

The boys walked back to their desks.

"It all makes sense now," Jake whispered. "Did you hear what Mr. Lavelle said? My grandfather arranged the art gallery field trip. He knew what would happen when the voyageur's choker and the paintings were brought together. My grandfather always encouraged me to draw as far back as I can remember, but I never took it seriously. This whole field trip was my grandfather's way of giving me the opportunity to experience our family's history, artistic talents and culture. It's now up me to decide what I'm going to do with it."

Jake paused, deep in thought. "I think I'll start with signing up for Mr. Lavelle's art classes and maybe even read about the Metis."

"Count me in," Pete said, impressed. "Just count me out if you feel like having any more *eye-blinking* experiences."

Vocabulary Builders

Avant – The avant sat in the bow of the canoe. He was responsible for setting the pace at which the paddlers traveled.

Bannock or Gallet – A type of bread introduced by the Europeans. It is a mixture of flour, salt, baking powder and lard.

Bois-Brûlés – The French name for the Metis, meaning burnt people.

Bourgeois – The agent who was hired by a fur trade company. He was responsible for a canoe brigade and the goods that were transported.

Chanteur – The singer was responsible for leading the men in songs so that they paddled in time to the music.

Gouvernail – The gouvernail or steersman sat at the stern of the canoe and was responsible for steering directions.

Metis – A French word meaning people with mixed blood.

Metis Sash – (cienture fleche or arrow sash) was originally woven entirely by hand and could be anywhere from 3.6 to 4.8 metres (12 to 16 feet). The original colours of the sash were: Green/Red/Tan/Brown. The Metis Sash was an important item due to its many uses that contributed to survival in the bush.

Michif - The language of the Metis people of Canada and the northern United States.

Pemmican - A mixture of meat (buffalo, moose, elk or deer) that has been ground into a powder and mixed with dried berries and rendered fat.

Portage - To travel over land carrying canoes and supplies from one lake or river to the next.

Red River Cart - A type of wagon made entirely of wood and pulled by horses or oxen. It was used by the Metis as a method of land transportation over the rough prairie.

Rubaboo - A stew using a chunk of pemmican boiled with vegetables.

Voyageurs - Men hired to transport trade goods and supplies between outposts to be used in the exchange for furs.

DEBORAH L. DELARONDE-FALK is a Metis writer who works in Duck Bay School in the community of Duck Bay, Manitoba. The stories in Metis Spirits were strongly influenced by her family genealogy, which can be traced through the Red River Settlement in the early 1800s to Acadia in 1633, when her great-grandfather arrived from France.

"All stories begin with an inspiration," Deborah says. "It is truly amazing and inspiring that the Europeans who came to Canada had the courage to try to live in unexplored territory and the wisdom to learn how to survive from the native people."

Deborah has written other books based on growing up in a Metis community – A Name for a Metis (1999), Little Metis and the Metis Sash (2000), Flour Sack Flora (2001), Flour Sack Friends (2003) and Friendship Bay (2004). All are available through Pemmican Publications.

· · · ·

KATHY MCGILL has more than 30 years of experience creating custom artwork. The majority of her painting is done in acrylic on an unlimited variety of canvasses, from rocks to living room walls. Kathy lives with her husband in rural Manitoba, where she runs her own business and enjoys visits from her grandson.